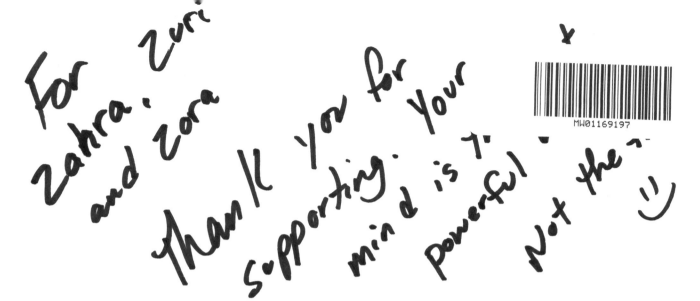

For Zahra, Zuri and Zora. Thank you for supporting. Your mind is t... powerful... Not the... :)

Medgar Malcolm Martin
The Petition

Written by Henry Charles

Medgar Malcolm Martin – The Petition

Written by Henry Charles

Illustrated by Eleonora Cali
Book cover/layout designed by B.R. Graphix LLC

ISBN: 979-8-9855243-5-2

DEDICATED TO MY BELOVED PARENTS
Marie-Solange & Henry Charles, Sr.

Henry Charles:
Medgar Malcolm Martin
The Petition

MEDGAR MALCOLM MARTIN

"I see they haven't installed a traffic light at the intersection of Beach Channel Drive and Stack Bundles Avenue," Malcolm said.

"Yeah, my mother did file a complaint with the city council. Something must be done," said Medgar.

"Are you two thinking what I'm thinking?" Martin asked.

Medgar, Malcolm, and Martin looked at each other and smiled.

Jenny, the principal, demanded that the students enter the school. The students followed the principal into the administration building. She was as upset as the children about the lack of a traffic light at the intersection after numerous pleas from the neighborhood to the city council. She dialed a number.

"I need a traffic light at this intersection!" shouted principal Jenny.

It seemed as if the entire school was in the main office. Principal Jenny ended the phone call with a few,

"Uh-huh."

"Uh-huh."

"Ohhhh! But that's not right."

"Uh-huh."

"Uh-huh." She sucked her teeth, then, "Psssssssh! Okay, thank you."

"So, what did they say?" asked Martin.

"That was my friend, a city council member," said Principal Jenny.

"She explained that it would take much more than a bad accident to put up a traffic light."

All of the students gasped. The main office was filled with a sense of defeat. The students' expressions changed.

"Aww, but that intersection is unsafe," said Aubrey Wyman-Grant.

"Ohhh-kaaay-okay," said Principal Jenny. "Make your way to the cafeteria. The pizza is on its way."

"Something has to be done," Malcolm told Medgar and Martin.

"I have a plan," Medgar said. "Give me a few moments, and we'll meet in the cafeteria. Let us eat and discuss things."

The three friends met in the cafeteria. There was fresh pizza everywhere.

"Mmm, pepperoni! My favorite!" said Medgar.

Malcolm grimaced. "How can you eat pork?"

"What?" Medgar said curiously.

The fats, toxins, and bacteria that are present in pork make it unclean, unhealthy, and harmful to humans. Malcolm carried on. Also, what good is it to eat something that spends its day rolling around in the mud?

Martin laughed as Medgar slowly put down his pepperoni slice and took one of Martin's plain cheese slices.

"So, what's the plan, Medgar?" Martin asked.

"I know how to get the city to install a traffic light," Medgar stated. "Of course, it'll take an army."

"I can get an army," Malcolm boasted.

"Good, because we're going to need one," Medgar said.

"So, what's the rundown, Medgar? How do we put this all together? " Asked Martin.

Malcolm clapped his hands three times quickly.

The entire cafeteria became silent and moved over to the table. "All right, everyone!" shouted Malcolm. "We witnessed another serious car accident at the intersection of Beach Channel Drive and Stack Bundles Avenue. Our parents all complained about this intersection, but nothing was done. Listen up! Medgar has a plan."

"Thanks, Malcolm," said Medgar.

Malcolm nodded. Medgar took a piece of paper from his pocket and unfolded it. He then placed the wrinkled piece of looseleaf paper on the table and smoothed it with his hand. There were handwritten instructions labeled from one to six. Medgar handed the piece of paper to Martin. The students gathered around the table as Martin read the steps aloud.

Step 1: Gather a group of concerned residents.

Step 2: Write your petition statement.

Step 3: Include space below the petition statement for signatures, addresses, and email addresses.

Step 4: Distribute the petitions to group members.

Step 5: Create a way where people can sign the petition 24 hours a day.

Step 6: Go to a town or city council meeting with your petition in hand.

"These are great. I will get started right away," said Steve.

"Not so quick, Steve," Malcolm said, seemingly upset. "When Mr. Josiah came outside, you were nowhere to be found. I watched how you left Medgar and Martin high and dry. We did not need you then and do not need you now."

"YEAH! **YEAH!** YEAH!"

The other kids shouted in agreement.

"Okaaay!" Steve said somberly with his head down, walking away from the group.

"All right, let's get back to the plan," Medgar said. "If we want to get things done, we need to get started as soon as possible."

That's what they did. Over the next few weeks, Medgar, Malcolm, Martin, and the kids from Far Rock Elementary school spread the word about the dangerous intersection. They designed banners and flyers. They then canvassed the rest of their neighborhood. They distributed flyers with information about their petition and where it could be signed. They went door to door, trying to reach everyone they could. They went to businesses, such as barbershops, hair salons, restaurants, the library, schools, churches, corner stores, supermarkets, doctor's offices, and bus stops, and asked everyone who was walking, running, driving, or biking around the neighborhood to sign the petition. Even the school staff pitched in, with teachers assisting with their preparations and lunch breaks.

"That's it!" exclaimed Medgar. "We have over ten thousand signatures. My mother arranged for us to speak at the next city council meeting. I will present our petition and signatures and request a traffic light." "Martin, we will need you to speak at the town meeting on our behalf," Medgar added.

"I am already on it," Martin said.

"Can you make sure everyone knows the date and time of the New York City council meeting, Malcolm?" Medgar asked.

"No problem," Malcolm answered. "However, it will not be that simple."

"What do you mean?" Medgar inquired. "We have everything we need. A dangerous intersection, tens of thousands of signatures. They cannot deny us or our demands."

When the New York City council meeting was set to take place, Medgar, Malcolm, Martin, and all the students were at the meeting along with their parents.

"Wow! I cannot believe we are here," Martin said. "This place is huge."

"Martin, we will need you to hit it big with one of your speeches," said Malcolm. "When you talk, people listen."

The kids laughed at Malcolm's comment. Martin nodded and gave Malcolm a fist bump. Far Rock Elementary School students entered the chambers and took their seats. The City Manager led the meeting. Also in attendance were the Assistant City Manager, City Attorney, Finance Director, Police Chief, Fire Chief, Public Works Director, and Planning Director.

The speaker stood up and said, "the first topic on today's agenda will be introduced by a community group petitioning for a traffic light."

"That is us," Medgar whispered to Martin and Malcolm.

As Martin approached the podium, the council members began to snicker and laugh. They thought it was amusing that a child was requesting a traffic light. Martin bravely approached the podium, flanked by Medgar and Malcolm, and read his speech. He described how his neighborhood was in dire need of a traffic light. He described how speeding cars exiting the expressway endanger other motorists and pedestrians. Martin received a standing ovation from the council members when he finished his speech.

However, Malcolm noticed that some council members were laughing instead of taking notes. He observed one council member say to another, "let us get to some more important business."

They moved on.

One day went by.

Two weeks went by.

Three months and five-car wrecks came and went, and no communication from the city council.

One day after school, Medgar, Malcolm, Martin, and most of the students from Far Rock Elementary stood on the corner of Beach Channel Drive and Stack Bundles Avenue. They waited to cross the street and watched cars accelerate as they exited the highway.

"I knew nothing was going to happen," said Malcolm.

"I cannot believe it," said Medgar. "All that work we put in, the signatures, the signs, all for nothing!"

"I stayed up all night writing that speech," Martin said disappointedly. Malcolm looked at the speeding cars and said, "we need to show them we mean business."

"How are we going to do that," said Trejur Guerrier.

"By holding up traffic," said Medgar.

"How?" said Layla Wynn. "These cars are going too fast."

Suddenly, a child dashes out into the middle of the street. It was Steve! A speeding vehicle comes to a halt inches away from Steve, bringing all other vehicles to a complete halt.

"The cars halted!" shouted Malcolm.

"Hurry, do not let them pass!"

The children formed a chain across the street, completely blocking traffic. Their plan worked! People in the neighborhood also joined in to help the kids. Drivers were confused as to why traffic. Traffic became so congested that cars were backed up all the way to the Verrazano Bridge.

As the day turned to night, the stranded drivers begged the kids to move, but they refused.

News vans arrived to see what was causing the traffic jam. A News reporter approached Medgar, Malcolm, and Martin.

"Why are you doing this?" the reporter asked.

Medgar stepped forward and cleared his throat, "we are here because this is a dangerous intersection. We did everything we could to get a traffic light. My community and I came together and petitioned for a traffic light."

"Then why are you here blocking traffic?" Another reporter interrupted.

"Our ten thousand signatures and our demands to get a traffic light fell on deaf ears," Malcolm said sternly. "We will not move until we are guaranteed a traffic light at this dangerous intersection."

The reporters walked away and continued filming the traffic jam, which could be seen affecting New Jersey. Malcolm approached Steve.

"Hey, that was a pretty dumb thing you did, jumping in front of the car like that."

"I know," replied Steve.

"But it got us here," said Medgar.

"I apologize if I hurt your feelings earlier," said Malcolm.

Malcolm and Steve shook hands.

A large fleet of black vehicles with dark-tinted windows parked at the corner a few moments later. The journalists rushed over to see who was in the vehicles. A security guard stood in front of an SUV's back passenger door. The door slowly opened. It was New York City Mayor Eric Adams. He knew what was causing the traffic jam and went directly to Medgar, Malcolm, and Martin. Cameras were flashing, people were cheering, and frustrated drivers were honking their horns.

"Gentlemen," he said to the three boys dressed in custom-fitted suits. "We can't have you here all night, despite how much I appreciate your peaceful protest. We must act in the best interests of our community. What can I do to help you get off the street?"

"All we ask, Mayor Adams, is that you install a traffic light at this intersection. Our school is here," Martin gestured to the school building. "Drivers exiting the highway speed through our neighborhood carelessly, making this intersection dangerous for children."

The mayor nodded.

"What can this neighborhood expect from you, Mayor Adams?" a reporter asked.

"They can expect me to do what is best for them," the mayor said proudly.

"These kids and this community needed to be heard; they went through the proper channels, and their needs were overlooked. We must congratulate these kids. They have determination, intelligence, and swagger!" The mayor continued. "I understand, and I apologize. I promise to have a traffic light up with a speed light camera to ensure drivers who speed exiting off the highway get ticketed."

The crowd erupted in a cheer. Medgar, Malcolm, Martin, and the crowd agreed to clear the street. The mayor waited for the crowd patiently to disperse and for traffic to start flowing before entering his motorcade.

Three days passed, and as the mayor promised, a traffic light was put up by the city along with a Speedlight camera.

"Malcolm, Martin, look!" shouted Medgar. "We did it!"
"You know, I had a dream about this," said Martin.
"Garrett Morgan would be proud," said Malcolm.

The End

About the Author

Best-selling author Henry Charles, Jr. was born in New York City and raised in Far Rockaway, Queens, the son of Haitian Immigrants. Henry's determination and belief in the importance of education afforded him the opportunity to attend Jackson State University, an HBCU, where he earned Dean's List status and received his Bachelor's Degree in Art and Graphic Design. He pressed on to earn a dual Master's Degree in General and Special Education, followed by a Master's in Instructional Technology from Touro College. His passion for knowledge manifested into a career as an educator in New York City for nearly two decades. While in the classroom, he realized that his students lacked the benefit of seeing themselves and their history in the content they read. His decision to write children's books led him to emerge as an author a decade ago, penning the play, *The Hologram Room*. Henry published his first novel, *Very Fine People,* in 2020, and earlier this year, Henry released his play, *The Hologram Room*, reimagined as a children's book. He went on to earn the title of best-selling author for his series *The Adventures of CAM: Full of All-Stars; Chairman Fred, Stuttering Henry* and was celebrated for becoming a best-selling publisher for *Big Brother,* and *It's Not Bedtime Yet*. Henry is married to his beautiful wife, Melanie. The two reside in Brooklyn, NY, with their son, Henry Charles III.

Visit **www.hiztorybookz.com** for more titles

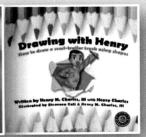

Made in the USA
Middletown, DE
11 March 2023

26439016R00031